W9-BSW-143

Where Is Jake?

Note

Once a reader can recognize and identify the 16 words used to tell this story, he or she will be able to read successfully the entire book. These 16 words are repeated throughout the story, so that young readers will be able to easily recognize the words and understand their meaning.

The 16 words used in this book are:

above	hi	Jake	to
down	hiding	out	under
eat	in	there	up
he	is	time	where

Library of Congress Cataloging-in-Publication Data

Packard, Mary.
    Where is Jake?/by Mary Packard; illustrated by Carolyn Ewing.
      p.   cm.—(My first reader)
    Summary: Two children search in many places for their dog, who stays just a step ahead of them
      Previously published by Grolier.
      ISBN 0-516-05361-2
      (1. Dogs—Fiction.) I. Ewing, C.S., ill. II. Title.
III. Series.
PZ7.P1247Wh 1990
(E)—dc20

90-30160
CIP
AC

Where Is Jake?

Written by Mary Packard   *Illustrated by Carolyn Ewing*

CHILDRENS PRESS ®
CHICAGO

Text © 1990 Nancy Hall, Inc. Illustrations © Carolyn Ewing.
All rights reserved. Published by Childrens Press®, Inc.
Printed in the United States of America. Published simultaneously in Canada.
Developed by Nancy Hall, Inc. Designed by Antler & Baldwin Design Group.

1 2 3 4 5 6 7 8 9 10 R 99 98 97 96 95 94 93 92 91 90

Where is Jake?

Is he hiding?

Is he in?

Is he out?

Is he under?

Is he above?

Is he up?

Is he down?

Jake? Jake?

Where is Jake?

Time to eat!

Hi there, Jake!